Dear Parent:

Congratulations! Your child is taking the first steps on an exciting journey. The destination? Independent reading!

STEP INTO READING® will help your child get there. The program offers five steps to reading success. Each step includes fun stories and colorful art. There are also Step into Reading Sticker Books, Step into Reading Math Readers, Step into Reading Phonics Readers, Step into Reading Write-In Readers, and Step into Reading Phonics Boxed Sets—a complete literacy program with something for every child.

Learning to Read, Step by Step!

Ready to Read   Preschool–Kindergarten
• big type and easy words • rhyme and rhythm • picture clues
For children who know the alphabet and are eager to begin reading.

Reading with Help   Preschool–Grade 1
• basic vocabulary • short sentences • simple stories
For children who recognize familiar words and sound out new words with help.

Reading on Your Own   Grades 1–3
• engaging characters • easy-to-follow plots • popular topics
For children who are ready to read on their own.

Reading Paragraphs   Grades 2–3
• challenging vocabulary • short paragraphs • exciting stories
For newly independent readers who read simple sentences with confidence.

Ready for Chapters   Grades 2–4
• chapters • longer paragraphs • full-color art
For children who want to take the plunge into chapter books but still like colorful pictures.

STEP INTO READING® is designed to give every child a successful reading experience. The grade levels are only guides. Children can progress through the steps at their own speed, developing confidence in their reading, no matter what their grade.

Remember, a lifetime love of reading starts with a single step!

Stephen Hillenburg

Based on the TV series *SpongeBob SquarePants,* created by Stephen Hillenburg,
as seen on Nickelodeon

© 2013 Viacom International Inc. All rights reserved. Published in the United States by
Random House Children's Books, a division of Random House, Inc., 1745 Broadway,
New York, NY 10019, and in Canada by Random House of Canada Limited, Toronto.
Nickelodeon, SpongeBob SquarePants, and all related titles, logos, and characters are
trademarks of Viacom International Inc.

Step into Reading, Random House, and the Random House colophon are registered
trademarks of Random House, Inc.

Visit us on the Web!
StepIntoReading.com
randomhouse.com/kids

Educators and librarians, for a variety of teaching tools, visit us at RHTeachersLibrarians.com

ISBN: 978-0-449-81875-6 (trade) — ISBN: 978-0-449-81876-3 (lib. bdg.)
Printed in the United States of America   10 9 8 7 6 5 4 3 2 1

STEP INTO READING®

STEP 2

nickelodeon

SpongeBob SQUAREPANTS

Party Time!

By John Cabell

Illustrated by Harry Moore

Random House 🏠 New York

It is
Squidward's birthday!
He gives himself
a new clarinet.

Squidward goes outside.

He plays

his new clarinet.

SpongeBob
is also outside.
He plays fetch
with Gary.

SpongeBob throws
a stick.
"Go get it, Gary!"
he says.

Gary brings
the stick back.
"Meow," says Gary.

Squidward puts
the clarinet down.

Oh, no!
SpongeBob accidentally
grabs the clarinet
and throws it.

Crack!

The clarinet breaks.

"I'm sorry,"

says SpongeBob.

"You have ruined
my birthday!"
yells Squidward.

SpongeBob must fix
Squidward's birthday.
"I will throw him
the best party ever,"
he says.

Patrick will help.
The party will be
at the Krusty Krab.

SpongeBob makes

a delicious cake.

Patrick blows
up balloons
and decorates
the Krusty Krab.

SpongeBob and Patrick
make a giant ice statue
of Squidward.

SpongeBob wraps
a special gift
for Squidward.
Everything is ready
for the party!

Mr. Krabs goes
to Squidward's house.
Knock, knock!

Squidward opens
the door.
"There is an emergency
at the Krusty Krab!"
says Mr. Krabs.

Squidward and Mr. Krabs
run to the Krusty Krab.

When Squidward
walks in,
everyone cheers.
"Surprise!" they shout.

"We are all here to wish you a happy birthday," says SpongeBob.

"I'm here for a Krabby Patty," says a customer.

SpongeBob gives
Squidward a gift.

It is

a new clarinet!

Squidward plays

a song.

Hooray!
Everyone claps.
Squidward bows.

Squidward thanks
SpongeBob.
"This was
a great birthday,"
he says.

Happy birthday,
Squidward!